be
resilient
be
you :)

Published by Collins
An imprint of HarperCollins Publishers
Westerhill Road, Bishopbriggs,
Glasgow G64 2QT

HarperCollins Publishers
Macken House,
39/40 Mayor Street Upper,
Dublin 1
D01 C9W8
Ireland

www.harpercollins.co.uk

978-0-00-870157-4

Printed in India by Replika Press

10 9 8 7 6 5 4 3 2 1

I dedicate this book to my wonderful
children Frankie and Annalise for
their resilience and their courage
in being entirely themselves and
pursuing their dreams.

With huge thanks to Jess Apps for
sharing the important 'know your
WHY' insight with me.

be resilient be you :)

THE TEENAGE GUIDE

Becky Goddard-Hill

illustrated by Josephine Dellow

being a teenager can be tough

Life is tough sometimes and the teen years can be particularly challenging. Your busy brain is rewiring itself, your hormones are surging, there may be pressure at school, and there are new relationships to navigate. You may, at times, feel overwhelmed and insecure and you might wonder how on Earth to get through it all.

There are many things you can do to help yourself discover and develop the strength you need to cope with any of the challenges you face.

It's time to grow your resilience.

what is resilience?

Resilience is the ability to cope with, and recover from, difficult experiences. It's all about developing robust coping skills and changing your thoughts, actions, and relationship strategies so that they help, rather than hinder you.

Resilient people face life's difficulties head-on by finding healthy ways to help themselves. They're able to adjust when life is hard and to find within themselves, or from others, the strength and support they need to get through.

Being resilient is a skill that you can learn and continue to develop throughout your life.

the 7C's of resilience

Dr Ken Ginsburg, a renowned paediatrician, developed a model called 'The 7 Cs: Building Blocks of Resilience' which set out the characteristics of resilient young people.

The 7c's are:

1. competence
2. connection
3. contribution
4. control
5. confidence
6. character
7. coping

In this book, you'll find strategies to help you feel stronger in each of these areas.

what's in the book?

The aim of this book is to help you bounce back from hard times, and to trust in yourself that you have the ability to cope when life is challenging.

It is split into four sections:

RESILIENT Relationships

Each of these sections looks at issues that impact your teen years and gives you guidance, rooted in science and research, to help you cope.

how to use this book

Use this book however you like. There is no particular order in which you need to read it. It contains 40 topics, some of which may be more important to you at one time than another. Please do try out the suggested activities included throughout the book, as just reading about something cannot replace the power of giving it a go.

And, if the strategies help you and you feel stronger as a result, please pass this book on to a friend. Connection and contribution are key to resilience and if this book can help someone else then it is a gift worth giving.

you will need...

 a notebook – for some of the activities to write, draw or make lists

 enthusiasm and an open mind – to try out the new ideas with positivity and optimism.

Resilience skills and strategies are easy to learn. They do, however, require regular practice and a can-do attitude, both of which are under your control.

Give these ideas a go and you will find that you absolutely can be more resilient, and this will help you tremendously your whole life through.

resilient
thoughts

:)

RESILIENT THOUGHTS

Your thoughts affect your feelings, and your feelings can affect your behaviour.

If you think to yourself 'I can't go to that party, it'll be a disaster' you will probably feel unconfident and worried. These feelings may lead to you cancelling.

If you think to yourself, 'I can give the party a go – it might be fun' you will likely feel more hopeful and braver, and you are more likely to show up, make new friends and dance for hours.

thoughts can be powerful

But just because you think something doesn't mean it's true, and you can question yourself if your thoughts aren't helping you. Are you catastrophising, and making something far worse than it is? Are you generalising, blaming others, seeing things only in black and white? With practice, you will stop believing everything you first think and start to challenge your thoughts or ignore them, and begin to think more positively.

Taking some control over your thoughts will change how you feel and what you choose to do. Learning how to do this takes time but it is absolutely possible. You are not 'fixed' in your way of thinking, you are growing and learning all the time.

In this chapter, we are going to take a look at how you can think in a more resilient way, how to recognise your strength and purpose, solve problems more efficiently, and be less of a dweller.

Changing and challenging your thoughts really can change your life for the better.

1 you can do hard things

Believe you can,
and you're halfway there.
Anonymous

incredible you

You are amazing.

Your friends and family know this, but what matters most is that you know and believe it wholeheartedly.

On the days you forget this, it is a good idea to take a moment and think about the strengths you possess that have got you this far. It's a fact... you have survived every hard thing you have ever faced.

Once upon a time you couldn't talk, walk, ride a bike, read or tie your shoelaces. In order to achieve any of these things you showed remarkable resilience.

You had to learn tricky skills, observe, practise, fail, practise again, get it wrong, and keep on trying! There will be many things you fail at first but eventually accomplish.

You have probably changed schools, made new friends, tried out for a team and didn't make it, or maybe you have lost someone you really cared about?

You have done (many) hard things and have coped with these hard things too.

tell your story

Have a think about something you found difficult and how you got through it. Write or tell someone else your story and focus on how you coped and what helped.

Remembering your day-to-day survival rate is 100%, even when what you are facing what feels beyond you, will strengthen you and help you move forward with confidence in yourself.

How you speak to yourself about your strength can make a huge difference to how strong you feel.

give it a go

Affirmations are short powerful statements we tell ourselves again and again until we believe them.

Tell yourself you want a drink, and your brain believes you and tells your body to pick up that cup and move it to your lips. Our brains believe what we tell them all the time.

Try telling your brain you can do hard things by repeating this statement...

I can do hard things.

Use a strong voice and repeat this affirmation three times every morning. With enough repetition you will begin to absorb and believe the message.

You know it's true, your past proves it, now simply say it again and again until your brain accepts it.

Believing you 'can' makes all the difference.

be resilient be you...

...and focus on your ability to cope with hard times.

2 look for the lesson

Life is a succession of lessons which must be lived to be understood.
Helen Keller, author and disability rights advocate

There are times (and EVERYONE has them) when you will feel that life is unfair, hurtful, sad, and confusing, and you will feel low.

refocus

It is important to pay attention to your emotions – they will provide all kinds of information to help you make sense of your experiences and decide what to do. But JUST focusing on how you feel can be overwhelming.

One way to build yourself up during tough times is to look for the lesson. A little time spent reflecting on what your experience is teaching you can add something positive and useful into the mix and help you move forward.

But how do you look for the lesson when all seems bleak?

You do it by intentionally refocusing your attention and reflecting.

Here are some questions you might like to explore. You may want to think these through, journal your responses or talk them over with a friend.

reflection questions

- What's something new I learned about myself during this time?

- Who has supported me?

- What would I do differently in the future?

- What can I learn from what I and others did in this situation?

- What has helped?

- If someone else was in my situation, what would I advise them to do?

You may want to work through these questions a few times and on different days, but give them your attention and the insights will come.

Hard times are painful and always unwelcome. But if you learn from them and use them as an opportunity to grow in some way you will gain something back that will stay with you forever.

Looking for the lesson in whatever your are experiencing can be enlightening. Here are some examples. Can you think of your own?

- I learned from my grandparents dying that it is important to tell people you love them when you get the chance.

- I learned from being ill to keep my body in great condition so it can cope with any challenges.

- I learned from losing a special friendship to expand my circle and nurture a wider friendship group.

be resilient be you...

...by looking for the lesson in tough times.

3 things you can control

Some things are up to us
and others are not.
Epictetus. Stoic philosopher

There are many things in life you cannot control, such as other people's thoughts, actions, and behaviour. Focusing too much on these things can make you feel helpless and frustrated.

but there is good news...

A great way to boost your resilience when you feel a lack of control is to refocus your attention onto the things you CAN control.

Fortunately, you can control many aspects of your life such as:

your words

- the words you use when you are angry
- the kindness and encouragement with which you talk to yourself
- your manners
- how you express gratitude
- saying what you need
- apologising
- saying 'I'll let you know' if you need time to think
- not saying 'yes' when you mean 'no'
- the compliments you give
- the encouragement you share

your actions

- spending time with people who make you feel good
- the music you listen to
- who you follow on social media
- asking for help
- taking care of your space
- helping out at home
- being a good friend
- prioritising what you need to do

your thoughts

- looking for positives from your day
- considering someone else's viewpoint
- accepting your imperfections
- learning from your mistakes
- setting yourself goals
- remembering how you have coped in the past
- who you share your thoughts with
- forgiving yourself

the science bit

Ancient stoic philosophers and modern psychologists agree that focusing on what you can control, rather than what you can't, reduces anxiety and can help you feel calmer and stronger.

give it a go

If you're dealing with a tricky issue in your life ask yourself:

What can I control in this situation? Make a list.

What can't I control in this situation? Make a list.

Now simply throw your 'can't control' list away.

Whenever you feel helpless, take a look at the 'can control' list, choose one thing from it and go do that. Reclaim your power and you will feel stronger.

be resilient be you...

...by focusing on the things you can control.

4 know your why

Your purpose in life is to find your purpose and give your whole heart and soul to it.
Anonymous

I have an amazing niece called Jasmine, who decided, along with her best childhood friend, that when they finished university, they would spend a year or more traveling the world together.

She began a Saturday job aged 15 and alongside acing her studies has worked ever since. She managed to save a lot of the money she earned towards her trip. She knew WHY she was working and WHY she was saving and ultimately this motivated her to keep focused, enthusiastic and on track.

And now?

Now she is now 23 and has her degree firmly under belt. She is currently in Australia with her friend at the end of a year-long trip having had the best time and many awesome adventures.

Knowing her WHY enabled her to make her dream a reality.

give it a go

Do you know your WHY?

Think about the things you do on a regular basis and ask yourself 'Why?'

- Why are you studying?
- Why do you go the gym?
- Why do you spend time on your hobbies?
- Why do you spend time with the people you do?

Writing down your WHY will reinforce it and strengthen your motivation and commitment.

If there is no great WHY, or your WHY is not healthy or does not benefit you or others, you might want to have another think about your choices – it might be time to change course.

But if your WHY is meaningful, hold onto it tightly, it will drive you forward.

A clearly defined WHY can be inspiring. It also stops you getting distracted, and helps you get past setbacks. In fact, knowing your why and feeling that you have a sense of purpose in life is so good that, according to researchers at Carleton University, it can even help you live longer!

be resilient be you...

...and know your WHY.

5 Blame

when it's not your problem

It is easy to think that everything that happens to you or goes wrong is somehow your fault. You can spend so much time worrying about how you caused situations or people to act in a certain way when actually, in some situations, it may be nothing to do with you.

Perhaps a friend asks to borrow your gym card because they don't have one. It's against the gym rules to give out your card so you say 'no'. Your friend tells you you've let them down and they'll never get fit now.

It's not your problem, so don't take on the blame.

Perhaps you could offer to run with them instead? Or tell them you get a free day pass once a month if they'd like to use that. What you DON'T need to do is feel guilty or worried. The problem of not being able to afford the gym is not yours to take on. It is theirs.

You can let it go.

when it is your problem

If every morning you get up with moments to spare and your grown-up has called you four times, you might feel annoyed at them for nagging you and feel stressed because you are running late. Whose problem is it?

Rather than blaming your grown-up or simply blaming yourself, view it as a problem to solve.

Taking responsibility when the issue or problem is yours will feel uncomfortable at first, but if you do take on that responsibility, it will help you feel stronger and less stuck.

the science bit

The famous psychiatrist Sigmund Freud suggested that blame makes people feel better because it brings relief from responsibility. But whilst blaming others for your issues might feel easier in the moment, it won't help you progress (or improve your situation).

Blaming others keeps you from seeing ways you can alter your behaviour or make the changes you need to.

the blame game

Researchers have found that the more you tell a story blaming someone else for something, the more you add to that story, so they become a bigger and bigger villain. Try not telling your story for a day and look at it quietly from different angles. You could even have a go at writing up your account of a situation, then attempting to write up a different viewpoint where you are not the victim.

If this is tricky, try asking someone neutral for their thoughts.

If you find you are at least partly to blame, then apologise and move forward doing things differently in future.

be resilient be you...

...by working out who a problem belongs to. If it's not you then let it go, and if it is you then tackle it head on!

6 this too shall pass

However long the night
the dawn will break.
African proverb

The saying: 'This too shall pass' comes from a folktale in which King Solomon sent his servant Benaiah to find a ring that, when worn, would make a 'happy man sad' and a 'sad man happy'. He asked him to return with it within six months, in time for Sukkot (a week-long Jewish holiday). He expected Benaiah to fail because he knew no such ring existed.

The night before Sukkot, Benaiah stopped and asked a jeweller if he knew of such a ring. The jeweller immediately inscribed a gold ring and gave it to Benaiah. To King Solomon's surprise he was presented with the ring, on which there were three Hebrew letters inscribed: a gimel, zayin, and yud, abbreviations for 'Gam zeh ya'avor'. In English, this means, 'This too shall pass.'

The quote tells us that no matter how dreadful (or how amazing) things are, they are only temporary.

bad times pass (hurray!)

Sometimes it feels that things will never get better. You might imagine you will never get over your disappointing GCSE results or your gorgeous dog dying.

But bad times do pass. Overwhelming loss, disappointment or worry will, in time, either leave you completely or will no longer be too big for you to carry.

Day always follows night and brighter days always come along, even if they take a while.

draw on your past

- Can you think back over your life so far and think of times of great stress, upset or worry?

- Can you think about how it resolved and what helped you through?

You may think you will never get past the huge feelings you have now, but your experience and your history shows you that you will, and that you always have.

Hold on even through the challenging times, all will be well.

good times pass too (but that's okay)

Just like bad times, good times pass too so it is important to appreciate them when they come along.

Next time you have a positive experience, capture the moment in your mind, or in a journal or a photo and retell the story of it often. Good memories can comfort and sustain you.

the science bit

Studies have shown that intentionally recalling happy experiences can help to disrupt negative thought patterns and reduce anxiety and stress, particularly in young people.

So, if you are feeling blue, look through your old photos, reminisce about happy days and give yourself a positive mental health boost.

be resilient be you...

...knowing that hard times pass and memories of good times will help you feel strong.

7 don't dwell or your problems swell

> You are not going to worry yourself out of a problem.
>
> Eckhart Tolle, spiritual teacher and self-help author

We all have low mood from time to time and we all have negative thoughts. But the very WORST time to pay attention to such thoughts is when you are already in a low mood. When you are feeling low, you are more likely to believe your negative thoughts and one may quickly lead onto another.

This is called spiralling.

how mood affects your thinking

Imagine Jon is in a good mood and gets his history paper back with a really low mark. 'Oops' he thinks 'that's not good'. But rather than staying with that thought, he quickly moves on to thinking about what he can do to improve. 'Maybe I should ask the teacher for a meeting to see what I can do to improve, or perhaps I need to spend more time on it.'

Because he is in a good mood, Jon can think of positive, useful steps forward.

Now imagine if Jon is in a low mood and he gets that exact same paper back. 'Oh no' he might think, 'What is wrong with me? This subject is too hard. Maybe I should give it up?'

When you are in a low mood, it is easy to get stuck in a loop of negative thinking and to distort how bad things are. These negative, distorted thoughts usually lead to negative feelings which just make our mood worse, and can then lead to negative behaviour (such as doing nothing or quitting).

the science bit

In his book *Stop Thinking, Start Living*, psychologist Richard Carlson, a world expert on happiness and stress reduction, extensively studied the habits of happy people.

As a result of his research, he advises you acknowledge your negative thoughts, but don't dwell on them.

He suggests you distract yourself with something positive in the here and now until your mood lifts (even just a little), then look again later at your worry. He has found that people are surprised about just how much more positive their approach to their problems are, and how much more manageable they seem when they have had a break from thinking about them.

Try it, I think you will be amazed.

give it a go

Moods pass all by themselves but if you want to speed things up, you can:

- get out in nature
- exercise
- watch something funny
- do a kind deed
- read a book
- spend time with uplifting people
- create something.

These actions will drag your mind away from negative thinking and ground you in the present moment where worries about the past and future don't exist.

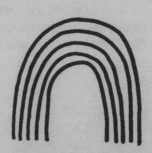

be resilient be you...

...and change your mood to change your mindset.

8 your no.1 fan

To fall in love with yourself is the first secret of happiness.
Robert Morley, actor

Your self-esteem is based on your opinions and beliefs about yourself.

If you have high self-esteem, other people's negative opinions of you will not shake you too much. They may make you feel a bit uncomfortable, but they won't topple you, because your roots will be strong.

Good friends and family members can be great cheerleaders, but realistically the one person who is going to be with you your entire life is you, so you need to be your own biggest cheerleader.

This doesn't mean you need to think you are perfect – after all you're a human being and that means you have flaws, weaknesses, and areas for growth. High self-esteem means that you love yourself and know you are worthy of a good life whilst still having areas you want to work on.

self-esteem in the teen years

As a child you probably had pretty high self-esteem and were praised for just painting a passable picture of a house! But, as you enter your teens, expectations on you may have risen that cause you to question yourself. Along with school pressures, social media, friendship, and relationship worries, and your physical and hormonal changes, it is common for self-esteem to wobble.

the science bit

A 2020 study of young people's wellbeing in the UK found that almost 50% of adolescents struggle with low self-esteem. That's a problem because lack of self-esteem can affect your mood, your confidence to try new things, and ability to tackle obstacles that come your way.

Resilience is often defined as the mental reservoir of strength that helps people handle stress and hardship. Knowing you are strong, capable and loveable will help give you that mental strength.

Let's work on your confidence!

give it a go

Reminding yourself regularly of your skills, talents and best qualities will help shore up your self-esteem.

Why not create a journal documenting these, or put together a scrapbook or a board of achievements that provides evidence of this?

Maybe you include a school report, some reflective writing, compliments you have received, certificates, photographs, or cards. Journal about kind things you do, when you have made someone laugh or tried something new.

You're fabulous – capture this and reflect on the evidence when you need a reminder, and your confidence needs a boost.

Higher self-esteem is linked with being both lovable and capable, so if you do struggle to find evidence, simply try doing something nice for someone else or working on a new skill. Both are going to make you feel a little stronger.

be resilient be you...

...by being your own biggest fan.

9 silver linings

The same wind that blows down your house shakes berries from the bushes.
Marci Ridlon, actor

A silver lining refers to the comforting thought of a positive aspect of a difficult situation. It's like finding a glimmer of light in a grey sky.

If something is getting you down and you feel a bit low, it can be pretty easy to miss the silver lining. Sometimes you need to intentionally search for it.

Looking for the silver lining doesn't mean you have to ignore your feelings of sadness or loss or hurt, but it does save you from catastrophising and thinking a situation is all bad.

the science bit

Looking for the silver lining is having an optimistic mindset,
and researchers have linked this to the ability to adapt
to, and cope with, stressful life events, lower levels of
depression and even lead to good physical health!

It's really good for you to look for silver linings!

'BUT' is a powerful word

'BUT' can help you see the brighter side of almost anything situation.

Here's how it works...

'I miss my best friend terribly now she's moved away BUT it will be great fun to visit her in her new city.'

'I got 5/10 on my maths test BUT that's better than last time and my teacher has set a session aside to help me.'

'I've been letting my room get in a terrible mess BUT I have a plan with Mum to declutter this Saturday which will make it easier.'

'My friends have started vaping and I'm feeling a bit left out BUT it's made me realise I know my own mind and I really value my health.'

Have a go at applying 'BUT' to something you currently find tough.

when times are really tough

You may not see the one good thing about your situation at the time. Perhaps it was the person who helped you through it, or your own powerful voice that spoke up and asked for help?

When times are tough it can be hard to see the silver lining but, as with your house keys or missing homework, if you look hard enough you'll eventually find what you are looking for.

be resilient be you...

...and always look for the silver lining.

10 coping with overwhelm

Keep it simple and focus on what matters. Don't let yourself be overwhelmed.

Confucius, philosopher

The word 'overwhelmed' is defined as 'having too much to do, feeling unable to cope'.

If you get overwhelmed by life sometimes, if it feels too busy, too much or too hard, don't worry – it's entirely normal to feel this way and happens to everyone from time to time.

Perhaps you'll have a big cry or a rest, regroup and carry on.

But what if you get stuck? Sometimes feelings of overwhelm can be hard to shake off and this can make coping with everyday life difficult.

This is when you need to take action.

it's okay to not be okay

Coping with overwhelm starts with being honest with yourself (or others) and saying, 'Right now I'm not okay.'

If you hide from your problems, they tend to just deepen. Once you admit you're not okay things begin to improve because you accept something needs to change.

From this point on you can take a break, lose some responsibilities, seek support or problem-solve the source of your overwhelm.

Acknowledging you have a problem is always the first step to solving it.

prioritise

What do you have on right now? Revision? A busy social life? Ten unanswered texts? Incomplete chores?

Too much is too much.

What can you lose out of your busy life? If you can let go of anything, now is the time to do so. Then look at what is left. Group tasks together where possible, such as answering texts, and decide the order in which you need to do things.

Making a list of priorities will help you feel more in control.

break it down

If you have a big project for school, or an extremely messy room to tidy, you may put off making a start because the task just feels too big.

Try breaking overwhelming tasks into small manageable tasks. For example, tidy your desk, empty your bin, then make your bed. Chunking a big job into lots of little ones makes it easier to get started. And, as you feel the satisfaction of completing one small task, you will be more motivated to carry on.

declutter

Messy spaces in your life make for messy spaces in your mind. Ten minutes spent sorting your school bag ensures you will find a pen; two minutes taking your cups downstairs gets your grown-ups off your case. These are quick, feel-good wins. And it is scientifically proven that a tidy space will help your mind feel less cluttered too.

But decluttering doesn't have to be physical. Mental decluttering and decluttering your schedule may mean you cancel a trip to the cinema, avoid scrolling, make a homework plan and turn off notifications by 8 p.m.

Simplifying your life gives you back time and space, and can make a huge difference to how overwhelmed you feel.

give it a go

What could you declutter today? Put a timer on for 20 minutes and just do it. Your overwhelm will lessen instantly.

be resilient be you...

...by taking action to reduce overwhelm.

resilient actions

:)

RESILIENT ACTIONS

you aren't just born resilient

Some people are naturally more sensitive than others and some people have harder life experiences which can make them feel less secure. Both these things can impact how strong you feel when you reach your teens.

BUT (and this is really important) you always have the power to grow your skills, increase your confidence and develop your courage and connections.

It takes effort, practice, and action to develop resilience – and it's in your power to do so.

neuroplasticity

Neuroplasticity refers to your amazing brain's ability to reorganise itself by creating new neurons and building new networks. You absolutely can become more positive, more optimistic, stronger, calmer and more secure.

Your brain is brilliant, it never stops changing and growing in response to the experiences you have. And the more you repeat experiences, the stronger any new neural pathways will become.

So, to be more robust in the face of life's challenges you need to take positive action and learn great coping skills – repeatedly.

take action

You don't need to wait till you feel strong and confident to make new friends and try new things. You just need to stride out into the world, give things a go, and watch your resilience grow as a result.

Feel the fear and do it anyway knowing you can handle it.

This chapter is full of ways to help you cope with life more easily, and by giving these ideas a go, you are going to feel stronger and more ready to face life's challenges.

Let's get started.

11 nature nurtures

You can cut all the flowers, but you can't keep spring from coming.
Pablo Neruda, poet, diplomat and politician

When life is difficult or upsetting, there is one thing you can always rely on to calm your nerves and make you feel that the world is ticking along just as it should.

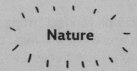
Nature

Nature has the most incredible power to reset your mood, soothe your nerves and clear your mind.

nature IS resilient

Resilience is the ability to bounce back, adapt, and recover from setbacks. Nature does this so well and taking time to watch natures' awesome resilience in action can inspire your own.

- Watching a tree blown about by the wind but standing firm and not being toppled is inspirational.

- Watching the Sun rise again after watching it sink the night before is motivational.

- Watching nature lose all its colour in the winter but blooming again in the spring gives hope.

You are part of nature – and you can do all this too – weather life's storms, rise after every fall, and always bloom again.

a sense of perspective

Nature puts our problems into perspective. It reminds us that there are bigger forces at work, and that we are just a small part of this Universe, and our worries are even smaller.

It's hard to look at the night sky or stand beside the ocean and feel we are anything but a small part of something much bigger.

the science bit

Researchers at Harvard Medical School discovered that spending just 20 minutes connecting with nature causes a big reduction in cortisol (stress hormone) levels in our bodies.

They found that the setting and time of day don't matter at all, so simply find your bit of nature whenever and wherever you can!

Other scientifically proven nature benefits include:

reduced depression

reduced anxiety

reduced stress

reduced mental fatigue

reduced anger and aggression

reduced experiences of pain

improved mood

improved sleep

improved confidence and self-esteem.

biophilia

Biophilia explains WHY nature makes you feel stronger.

'Biophilia', means 'love of life and the living world' and the term was coined by biologist, E Wilson in 1984. He believed that, since we evolved in nature, we have a biological need to connect with it.

In ancient times it provided us with the food, warmth and shelter we needed. Wilson believes the reason we feel so safe and calm in nature is because we innately love and feel protected by the things that once helped us survive.

Poets, philosophers, gardeners, and scientists all agree: Whatever the problem, nature is the answer.

give it a go

Try a few of the following for 20 minutes each day to make you feel amazing:

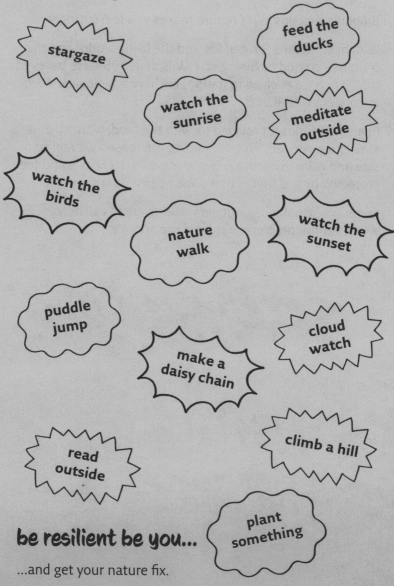

stargaze

feed the ducks

watch the sunrise

meditate outside

watch the birds

nature walk

watch the sunset

puddle jump

cloud watch

make a daisy chain

read outside

climb a hill

plant something

be resilient be you...

...and get your nature fix.

12 study smarter

School is tough, but so are you.
Becky Goddard-Hill

When studying, you will probably face various challenges no matter how studious you are. You might find your workload overwhelming, organising your notes hard, or tests anxiety-inducing.

These challenges are common to all students, but that doesn't make them any less frustrating.

Let's take a look at the 7C's of resilience and see how they can help you thrive in your studies.

1. connection

Who is your support network, who are the best study buddies, teachers, people in your home, to help you when studying is a problem?

Identifying strong connections can help you get over any issues far more quickly, as well as helping you feel supported and less alone.

Can you make a list?

2. coping

Avoidance or procrastination, as coping strategies, may feel good temporarily, but ultimately both of these will affect your chances of success and increase your worries.

Breaking down tasks into small, manageable chunks makes them more achievable. Make yourself a study or homework planner and colour off the sections you have completed. Seeing what you have achieved is already a confidence-boost. Slot free time, and maybe even some treats, into your planner too so you get regular breaks.

If you panic in exams, try practising past papers under exam conditions and learn to breathe deeply.

Do whatever you can to help yourself cope.

3. confidence

The more you take action
to overcome obstacles in
your way, the more your
confidence will grow, and
you'll feel calmer about your
studies. So, plan, prepare, access support, knuckle down,
and get organised.

It does wonders for your confidence to be on top of things.

4. courage

Courage is not a lack of fear, courage is acting despite fear.
It's admitting you don't understand, have fallen far behind
or chosen the wrong course, and then doing something
about it.

Courage makes all the difference to how things work out,
so take action – you will be glad you did.

5. competence

The more you study the more you will know, but it is
important to do it right.

Go to that revision skills class, or read about different
techniques, so you get the best results for the work
you put in. As your study skills grow, you will
feel more competent and as a result you
will feel increasingly confident.

6. control

You can't control your
exam questions, whether
you get ill mid-course, or how easy you find algebra.

Focusing on things you can't control can make you feel
helpless.

If you want to increase your chances of getting through
hard times whilst studying, focus on what you CAN
CONTROL. For example, you can revise, and you can
practise. Put all your energy into these areas.

7. character

A fixed mindset says, 'I am not good at maths, there is no
point trying.' It's not helpful.

A growth mindset believes in your power to make progress,
so would say 'I'm working on improving my maths skills all
the time.' This is much more helpful!

Making an effort to improve areas where you struggle is the
sign of a strong character and will make a huge difference
to how you approach studying setbacks (and life in general).

All areas related to your studies will be easier and more
successful if you work on the 7 C's of resilience.

be resilient be you...

...and study smarter.

13 positive incentives

Show me the incentive and
I will show you the outcome.
Charlie Munger, businessman and philanthropist

An incentive is a reward for a completed task.

It is a great idea to incentivise yourself when there is
something challenging, difficult, or even boring that you
want or need to achieve.

Incentives can help you push through tricky times.
And, rather than wait for someone else to recognise your
achievements and reward you with a 'well done' or a day off
your chores, it is a good idea to take matters into your own
hands.

when, then

Imagine you have homework, and you also want to hang out with your friends. You could say to yourself 'I'll hang out with my friends first and after that I'll do my homework.'

The problem with this scenario is that the fun thing will be over first and then you're simply left with your homework. It hardly encourages you to power through an essay when there is nothing waiting at the end of it.

If you say to yourself WHEN I have done my work, THEN I'll hang out with my friends, you are giving yourself a clear reason to get on and do it.

Using when and then is powerful. Making a deal with yourself that WHEN (you have done the hard thing) THEN (you get the reward) gives you a focus and a reason to complete your task.

Here are some examples:

- 'When I have finished tidying my room, then I'll make myself a hot chocolate.'

- 'When I have saved four weeks pocket money, then I will buy those earrings.'

- 'When I've rehearsed my lines, then I'll listen to my favourite podcast.'

the science bit

According to psychologists, who have studied the power of incentives, these three things can help:

Creating a reward that is important to you
If your reward isn't strong enough, it is likely you won't feel very motivated.

Engaging in visualisation
Closing your eyes and imagining receiving the reward. How it might feel can motivate you into action.

Making it achievable
Promising yourself a TV break after an hour and a half of studying is much more motivating than after four hours!

give it a go

Think of a task you have put off because it is tricky, boring or challenging. Schedule it in and write down a direct reward for completing it and write it up like this.

Reflect afterwards on how much more focused you were. Use 'when and then' whenever you have something tough to do. Reward yourself for a job well done.

be resilient be you...

...and create positive incentives.

14 *avoidance*

> ## Either you run the day, or the day runs you.
> Jim Rohn, author and motivational speaker

Do you write a 'to do' list – a list of all the things you want and need to achieve in your day?

They can be really useful.

'to do' lists help you achieve more

Studies have shown that people perform better when they write down the details of what they need to do. 'To do' list writers are more like to make a start, stay focused and not get distracted.

'to do' lists make you happy

Scientists at Harvard Medical School have found that 'The satisfaction of ticking off a small task is linked with a flood of dopamine.'

Dopamine is a brain chemical involved in motivation and pleasure. The dopamine hit you get by completing a task on your list will feel so good it will spur you on to complete your next task too.

So, ticking something off your 'to do' list keeps you both happy and motivated.

'to do' lists ease your worries

A study by professors Baumeister and Masicampo from Wake Forest University showed that, while tasks you haven't done can distract and overwhelm you, making a plan to get them done frees you up from this anxiety.

So, to sum up: 'to do' lists impact motivation, help you feel happier and less stressed and increase your achievements.

What a great return for just five minutes spent writing a list!

what to put on your 'to do' list

Include a variety of quick and easy tasks and longer, more tricky ones. Mix it up to keep it interesting and so you don't get bored!

You might want to include things like:

1. exercise
2. write my essay
3. call a friend
4. empty the dishwasher
5. walk the dog
6. do my affirmations
7. practise guitar.

give it a go

Have a go at making a 'to do' list each morning this week and notice how much more you have achieved by the end of each day and how you feel.

a quick win

Put 'Make to do list' the last thing you include on your list, so that you can immediately mark something off. So satisfying!

And if you don't get something done – no worries pop it onto tomorrow's list and know you'll get there in the end.

a 'ta-da!' list

If you forget to start the day with a 'to do' list, consider making a 'ta-da!' list instead. Look back on your day and list all the tasks you have completed. It will help you see just how much you have achieved and will strengthen your self-belief.

be resilient be you...

...and write a 'to do' list to you help you feel focused, capable and in control.

15 take an umbrella

> There is only one corner of the universe you can be certain of improving, and that's your own self.
>
> **Aldoux Huxley, writer**

a resilient rose

Roses are fragile, beautiful and fragrant flowers and are as attractive to insects as they are to us. But roses bloom brilliantly and survive because they also grow thorns, and this stops them being eaten.

Just like a rose, you can protect yourself from tough times by small, deliberate actions that are SO worth the effort.

'Being practical' may sound a bit boring but it absolutely makes hard times easier.

help yourself!

Imagine it's pouring with rain, and you are heading out to meet with friends in your new outfit, feeling good.

You can't stop the rain, but you can CHOOSE to minimise its impact with an umbrella. You may not think that looks cool, but you will arrive looking your best and be dry and comfortable the entire time you are out.

You can help and protect yourself in so many ways, by making smart choices like this and taking action.

the science bit

Psychologists have found that writing down the pros and cons of several options can help teens tackle a problem with logic, rather than basing their decision on emotion alone.

Emotions are strong in your teen years so anything that helps you think logically is a win!

give it a go

Below are a host of scenarios that might cause you to wobble, feel worried or upset.

Think about a small practical action you could take in each situation that would help you to help yourself. Use an action word in all your answers. If you struggle, think what you would tell a friend to do.

- You have a hard test coming up.

- You don't understand your English assignment.

- You have try-outs for the football team.

- Your sister keeps borrowing your clothes.

- You have a bus trip with school and are worried about who to sit with.

- The person you walk to school with is always late.

- You keep yawning by teatime.

- You spend hours on your phone and your grown-up keeps complaining.

- You keep losing your keys and getting told off for it.

- You feel run down and keep getting colds.

- Your friends keep teasing you.

Taking practical actions to help yourself gives you a much better chance of coping with hard things, and minimising their impact.

Take small steps consistently to help yourself and you will gain confidence with each new task you accomplish. Self-preservation will become a habit.

be resilient be you...

...and carry an umbrella!

16 glimmers

> Joy is what happens to us when we allow ourselves to recognise how good things really are.
> **Marianna Williamson, author and politician**

A glimmer is a mini moment or experience that brings you a feeling of joy or safety, and prompts your nervous system to calm down. The opposite is a trigger, something that makes you feel anxious and fearful, like lightening flashing or someone shouting.

Triggers put your body on high alert and create stress. Glimmers do the exact opposite.

Common glimmers include things like:

- feeling the warmth of the Sun on your face
- the smell of cut grass
- seeing a double rainbow
- your favourite song coming on the car radio
- the first sight of the sea on your holiday
- your cat curling up in your lap
- watching a leaf fall
- hot chocolate on a cold day.

Glimmers make you feel the world is okay, even if just for a fleeting moment.

the science bit

According to clinical psychologist, Perpetuia Neo, glimmers are micro-moments of goodness that help your body to discharge the build-up of cortisol (the stress hormone) from previously stressful situations, so you can return to a calm state.

And the more you look for glimmers the more you will find them due to our brilliant brains' Reticular Activating System (RAS).

The RAS works like a filter – it looks at the enormous amount of information happening in your world and delivers the pieces it considers most important into your awareness. For example, if you buy a great new pair of trainers, you will probably start to spot others who are wearing them too. Your clever brain scans for what you are focused on and presents it to you.

So, if you intentionally look for glimmers, you will find yourself becoming aware of more and more and you will feel happier and calmer as a result.

give it a go

You now know that finding glimmers will make you feel good and will encourage you to look for more, but being aware of your glimmers is the first step.

- Tune into your five senses to explore all that you are experiencing in the moment.

- Keep a glimmer diary and record your glimmers to cement them in your mind.

- Ask someone in your home to go on a glimmer journey too and share their glimmers each day with you.

Glimmers are great for your mental health. They will encourage you to seek out positive experiences and reduce your stress, so that you feel stronger and more able to cope with challenging times.

be resilient be you...

...by seeking out and focusing on glimmers.

17 try new things

When was the last time you did something for the first time?
Anonymous

Trying new things may sound scary, and stepping out of your comfort zone might initially feel hard, but the more you try new things the less fear of failure will bother you.

Some things you try you might love or be great at, some things might need more work or not be to your liking at all.

You will come to see that all of that is okay because when you have a life full of new experiences, finding one or two things tricky or not for you won't be such a big deal.

Expanding your world does not have to be dramatic, you can do it one tiny step at a time.

the science bit

In a huge review of a range of resilience research by the American Psychological Association, trying new things was found to be one of the top resilience-promoting ways a young person can help themselves.

give it a go

Here are ten tiny suggestions for expanding your world:

- try eating something you have never eaten before
- try eating lunch with someone new at school today
- try a brand 'new to you' skill (juggling/origami/baking)
- listen to a new genre of music

- take a new style of book out the library

- pop to the charity shop and buy a new top in a colour you wouldn't normally wear

- watch a programme you wouldn't normally watch

- take on a task at home that you wouldn't normally attempt

- walk a new route home from school/college

- learn how to sign your name and say hello in British Sign Language (BSL).

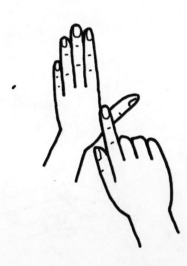

You may not enjoy the new things you try or ever want to do them again, but they may light a spark that ignites a fire in you. And yes, it may feel uncomfortable at first. As research professor and author Brene Brown puts it, 'You can have courage, or you can have comfort, but you can't have both.'

Even when things don't go as planned, taking on a new challenge proves to yourself that you are courageous. And attempting new things spurs you on to try other things and to take on more challenges.

You will start to think of yourself as brave, and think 'If I can do this, I can do that too.'

So, give it a go today (and every day).

be resilient be you...

...and try something new.

18 have lots of baskets

You have as many options as you give yourself.
Kasie West, author

When you think about it, putting all your eggs in one basket is actually very risky.

The phrase originated in the 1600s when farmers used baskets to collect eggs from their chickens. If a farmer put all the eggs in one basket and that basket broke, all the eggs would be lost, and they would have nothing to sell or to eat. It would be a disaster!

It is always a good idea to have wider options.

keep your options open

Cara dreamed of being a professional gymnast and had attended practice three times per week since she was small. It took up a lot of her time. But Cara was smart: dedicated as she was to gymnastics, she kept her options open. She had a go at other sports too and found she also enjoyed running, swimming and netball. Despite years of training in her early teens, after much thought she decided gymnastics was no longer for her.

This could have been a huge loss for her, but because she had tried other sports she knew she enjoyed, Cara decided to now explore these more deeply. She found her resilience in the fact she had options and could take her skills forward.

Cara now plays netball for Wales and loves it far more than she ever loved gymnastics!

Not putting all your eggs in one basket doesn't mean you spread yourself so thin that you are unfocussed or over-stretched. It does mean you explore your options and keep your mind open to other possibilities.

the problems with single focus

It is good to have goals and to show commitment in all aspects of life, but not everything in life goes to plan.

According to a study by the University of Pennsylvania, people who are flexible and willing to change their plans are more likely to achieve their goals.

This suggests that it's important to not be completely fixated on just one thing, so check yourself – in which areas are you single-focused and what can you do about it?

ask yourself this:

- If you only have one good friend, what happens if you fall out?

- If you have one hobby, what happens if you decide it's not for you?

- If you only consider one career, what will you do if you don't get the exam results you need?

Put your eggs in a few baskets and then if one drops and the eggs break, you will still have others to enjoy. This will help you cope with life's challenges and could lead on to better things.

be resilient be you...

...and don't put all your eggs in one basket.

19 name it to tame it

The best way out is always through.
Robert Frost, poet

Denying or hiding how you really feel may seem like a good way to avoid stress and heartache, but wearing an emotional mask doesn't work.

Feelings arise for a reason and if ignored they simply fester, and things may get worse. It is useful to consider your emotions and what (if anything) you want to do about them.

Some feelings just pass and that's okay, perhaps you are mildly irritated, and nothing needs to be done. Some feelings will stick around though, or feel so strong or uncomfortable you know they are giving you information you need to act on.

name it to tame it

A term psychologists often use in relation to feelings is 'name it to tame it'.

Naming your emotions kickstarts your prefrontal cortex (the thinking part of your brain). This helps you feel calmer immediately.

This technique was first identified by psychiatrist, Dr Daniel Siegel. He discovered that naming intense emotions signals the brain to send soothing neurotransmitters to the amygdala (the emotional part of your brain). These transmitters stop your feelings overwhelming you.

the science bit

You might wonder why in your teen years you have such incredible highs, and lows such as anger and anxiety?

During your teens, your amygdala is super sensitive, so your feelings are stronger. Your sensible prefrontal cortex isn't fully developed until your twenties, and this explains why your feelings are often intense and why, when they are, it can be hard to think clearly.

you don't have to talk

Some people find it easy to talk about how they feel, but if you don't that's okay. Instead, you could:

- write
- draw
- sing
- make art
- create music
- dance.

One of these activities might help to give a name to, and make sense of, your emotions. Do whatever works for you, but do express how you feel.

distance

Naming your emotions creates a healthy distance between you and your reaction.

Walk away if you need to, take your time, you have options.

Be curious about your feelings and respond to them with care if you feel it is right to do so. For example, you have a right to be angry if someone is mistreating you – don't ignore that emotion. You can choose how BEST to respond (not react) to that anger by acknowledging it, cooling down and considering your options.

If you get stuck in your negative emotions, reach out for help from family, friends, school, your GP, or an outside support helpline. It can really help to talk.

give it a go

Next time you feel a big emotion take these steps:

1 Exhale deeply several times, drop your shoulders and let out a long breath.

2 Now try and name what you are feeling in simple words to kickstart your thinking brain.

3 Ask yourself if you want to do anything about this emotion or just let it pass. If you do want options wait until you are calm and then explore them.

You are NOT your feelings, you are experiencing a feeling and you are in control.

be resilient be you...

...and express how you feel.

20 let music move you

Wake up, live your life and sing the melody of your soul.
Amit Ray, author

I have asked many teens what helps them feel stronger and more resilient, and music almost always tops the list.

Music is a super speedy way to quickly change your mood.

science bit

Did you know that emotions are contagious?

Our clever brains contain mirror neurons that pick up and reflect the moods of those around us, and researchers have found that we catch the mood of a piece of music in just the same way that we do the moods of other people.

If you play a happy song, you will feel happier, and if you play a sad song and really listen, you might find yourself in tears.

So, if you want to feel stronger and more confident, it makes sense to listen to songs that inspire you.

give it a go

Why not make yourself a mood boosting playlist and give it a blast if you are feeling low?

All sorts of songs can make you feel more confident. My great uncle Harold used to listen to marching bands to help him feel ready to get on up and get on. Whatever you choose will be unique to you, but it's always fun and refreshing to mix up your listening.

Why not ask others of all ages to share their top songs for making them feel strong. You might find some new brilliant tunes.

Here are some confidence-boosting songs to get you started:

1. The Greatest – Sia
2. My Shot – Hamilton Soundtrack
3. Run the world – Beyoncé
4. Born This Way – Lady Gaga
5. Roar – Katy Perry
6. Fight Song – Rachel Platten
7. Fighter – Christina Aguilera
8. Flowers – Miley Cyrus
9. This Is Me – Keala Settle
10. Stronger – Kelly Clarkson

It doesn't matter whether the songs you listen to are cool or current, what matters is they boost your resilience. Go make your list and use it whenever you need help feeling stronger!

Having a little dance too or doing a workout as you listen will also lead to an improved mood.

be resilient be you...

...and play music that makes you feel strong.

21 hobbies

Make the most of today. Shake yourself awake. Develop a hobby. Let the winds of enthusiasm sweep through you. Live today with gusto.
Dale Carnegie, writer and lecturer

In your teens, the pressures of school and your increasing desire to spend time with friends (or online) may mean you have less space in your life for outside hobbies and interests.

Yet hobbies bring so many benefits, that it is important to make time for them. They enable you to take a break from the pressures of school, family and friends and allow you to indulge your own unique interests.

flow

In doing something you truly enjoy, you will often get into a state of flow and really 'be in the moment' rather than worrying about the past or what's happening next. Being 'in the moment', fully focused on what you are doing, is a brilliant way to give your busy mind a break.

Nearly all hobbies help you develop skills that enable you to feel more capable, knowledgeable, or accomplished the more you practise. This is great for your self-esteem and helps you feel stronger.

Hobbies may feel like fun, but they continually help you to grow and develop.

the science bit

Hobbies are good for your mental health too.

A study from the Society of Behavioural Medicine found that people who take part in leisure activities have fewer negative emotions and are less stressed. They found that people's heart rates are literally lower when they engage in their hobbies.

follow your own interests

Sometimes it may feel easier just to do the same hobbies as your friends. But try to explore your own interests and find what you love. It may feel scary to try something new on your own, but if it's something you are drawn to, take your courage in your hands and give it a go.

hobbies can be social

Social hobbies, like tennis or drama, sometimes bring new relationships into your life. Shared interests make bonding with others easier and outside friendships can be a huge blessing if school friendships or home life go through testing times.

hobbies can be solitary

It is healthy to spend time by yourself too, whether reading, playing your guitar or sketching. The wonderful thing about a solitary hobby is that you are only relying on yourself to make it happen. You don't need to wait for anyone else to be available, or for scheduled times, for it to happen.

Solitary hobbies also give you a complete break from other people, which everyone needs from time to time.

Hobbies are brilliant!

give it a go

Have a think about a solitary hobby you would like to pursue. It could be anything from writing a rap song to becoming a star baker. Give it a go this week.

be resilient be you...

...find what interests you and make time for it.

22 journaling

A journal is your completely unaltered voice.

Lucy Dacus, singer-songwriter

Do you find yourself saying things so you fit in, so you please someone, or don't make them cross? This is completely normal. Everyone alters their voice from time to time, but it is so refreshing to be able to be completely yourself and say what you really think and feel.

Writing a journal enables you to speak freely and from the heart.

Unlike a diary, it's not a daily instalment of what you have done, but a space where you can write down and explore what's really on your mind.

Through journaling you are forced to slow your busy brain down and give your thoughts and feelings space to exist without being censored. This can help you gain insight into what you are experiencing and help you make better decisions.

the science bit

Bottled up feelings will make you feel stressed and eventually burst out anyway – often in an unhelpful or inappropriate way. Journaling gives you a place to express these feelings and this can help you feel calmer and stronger.

A 2018 study from Pennsylvania State University, involving 70 adults with anxiety, found that journaling for 12 weeks significantly reduced their mental distress. Long-term journaling was also associated with much greater resilience.

positive prompts

As well as using it as a place to outpour you challenging emotions you can also use a journal to increase your joy!

Did you know your brain has something called a 'negativity bias'? This means that you are more likely to give time and attention to negative things than positive ones. To increase your brain's ability to find the positives you have to seek them out more often. So do make sure when you are journalling you add in the good stuff too.

Try to include entries that answer the following questions:

What are you grateful for today?

What went well today?

What made you laugh?

Who has supported you today?

Gratitude is POWERFUL and helps you look at life differently. Make it part of your day and ask yourself frequently 'What went well?' – talk about it a lot too!

anything goes

Journaling doesn't have to be neat. Some people draw, stick in pictures, mind-map, doodle or just write – anything goes! Don't worry about your spelling and grammar either.

a safe space

Your journal is a place you can visit at any moment to express your inner thoughts, hopes, and fears, without worrying about being judged. Keep it away from prying eyes and treasure it.

give it a go

Journaling requires only pen, paper and attention, can be done anywhere and is free and therapeutic. It is the perfect well-being tool. Grab a notebook and get started!

be resilient be you...

...and start journaling!

23 brilliant books

Books are a uniquely portable magic.
Stephen King, author

Books are often the greatest source of comfort and inspiration in challenging times. Books are friends that never let you down and you can pick them up whenever you need them.

If you aren't a reader, then I suggest you practise reading little and often, until it flows more easily. Audiobooks are great too and you can listen to them as you walk.

the science bit

Reading is amazingly good for you, especially if you are feeling anxious or overwhelmed.

In fact, a study at the University of Sussex found that reading can reduce stress by up to 68%.

the benefits of books

Books can:

- inspire you – stories of resilient people, or books about a passion you might like to pursue, can be inspirational

- relax you – fiction enables you to escape for a while into a different world

- represent you – reading about someone with similar issues to you can make you feel seen and less alone

- introduce you to something new – reading can open your mind and expand your world, perhaps you will learn about another culture, or a disability you weren't aware of?

- motivate you – books can motivate you to try new hobbies or consider a career

- educate you – books can teach you about your changing body, or how to speak another language

- help you explore who you are – books can help you work out your values and identity in a safe space.

Books can nourish and support you in so many ways.

reading well

Reading Well for Teens is a list of books collated by The Reading Agency who worked with teens and wellbeing experts to choose books to help young people manage their emotions and cope with difficult times.

Ask at your library to see the collection or look online.

give it a go!

Take a visit to your library this week and if you aren't already, become a member. You will gain free books on tap and access to librarians who can help you find any book you wish for.

While you're there, check out a type of book you would never normally read, perhaps a graphic novel or a poetry book, a recipe book or a travel guide? You may just find you like it.

be resilient be you...

...and read!

24 positive
problem-solving

> Not everything that is faced can be changed. But nothing can be changed until it is faced.
> **James Baldwin**

Whatever the problem is the most important thing to do is to ask yourself the question – is there anything I can do about this?

In almost every situation there is some action you (or someone else) can take to solve or lessen the problem.

Being resilient in the face of a problem means taking action, getting support and thinking creatively about what you can do, not what you can't.

a problem shared is a problem halved (sometimes)

It can be tempting to moan endlessly about your problems, but moaning about your issues doesn't solve them and can increase your focus on what's wrong, rather than how to put it right.

Complaining you don't understand your maths homework to your maths-hating sister is wasted energy. Asking your maths teacher or your maths-genius classmate to help you is far more useful.

Sharing problems can be helpful but do consider carefully who you turn to... are they the right person to help?

small problems

Small problems such as misplaced homework or a one-sided crush may be frustrating, but try not to catastrophise. Think logically about how big this issue really is by scoring it out of 10 – it will help you keep perspective.

big problems

Big problems, such as very dark thoughts or being bullied, need to be acknowledged and addressed promptly. Left untackled these problems could deepen and have long-term impacts. This is the time to turn to a trusted adult to help you consider your options. There are always options.

the science bit

Neuroscientists have discovered the teenage brain develops unevenly. The emotional area of the brain develops well ahead of the pre-frontal cortex (the area responsible for impulse-control). This is why in your teen years you may find you react to a problem rashly, rather than think it through first.

pause for problem solving

When you have a problem, it is important to stop and think about the best way to respond. If someone sends you a nasty text and you fire one straight back, things will only escalate. Reduce impulsive reactions to problems by visualising a big stop sign, then take a deep breath, calm yourself down and think through your options.

give it a go

Try tackling one of your current problems using the adapt acronym below.

Attitude – adopt a positive, hopeful attitude towards your problem

Define – define your problem clearly

Alternatives – identify a variety of actions to overcome your problem

Predict – predict the outcome of each of the actions above and choose the one you think is most likely to succeed

Try out – try out the action. If it doesn't work just start again at **A**.

Keep practising your problem-solving skills so you feel increasing capable and confident about coping with wherever challenges arise.

be resilient be you...

...and use positive problem solving.

resilient bodies

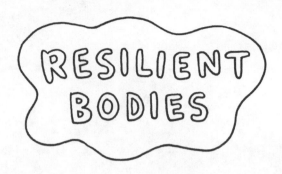

mind-body connection

Your mind and body are completely interlinked and have a direct impact on each other, affecting your health and wellbeing. If your body is tired, your mind will feel tired too and if you have stressful thoughts, your body will become tense.

Understanding this mind body connection encourages you to listen to and take great care of your body.

In this section of the book, we will take a look at ways to look after your body that will make you feel stronger and calmer both physically and mentally so that you can live your best life.

physical resilience

Taking action towards a healthier life will help you build physical resilience. Physical resilience is your body's ability to adapt to challenges, maintain energy, and recover well from setbacks.

It doesn't mean you'll never have a sleepless night, get poorly, or eat five easter eggs in a row, but it DOES mean you will bounce back from that with energy, determination and healthy habits.

Building a more resilient body is down to the effort you put in and it is completely worth that effort.

If you take care of your body, it will take care of you.

25 eat well

> Take care of your body. It's the only place you have to live.
>
> Jim Rohn, author and motivational speaker

Eating well protects you against illness, gives you energy and helps your body grow strong and healthy. It is a powerful way to help yourself feel strong.

the science bit

In your teens, your body goes through rapid growth and change, and it is likely that your appetite will increase. Your height, weight, muscle mass, and bone density increase, and organs like the heart and brain continue to grow.

You need to feed your growing body all the good stuff!

treats

Sugary or fatty foods such as chocolate, crisps, and biscuits are high in calories but contain few nutrients. They won't fill you up and will often leave you craving more.

You wouldn't feed a puppy endless treats, you'd give them food that nurtured their growth.

Do the same for yourself.

what you need

The British Nutrition Foundation advises teens do the following daily:

have breakfast

Many teens skip breakfast for a variety of reasons. But it matters. By the time you wake up, it is hours since you last ate and your breakfast boosts your energy, helping you face the day.

(If you are unable to eat something before you leave the house in the morning, remember that most schools have breakfast food available – have a chat with your teacher.)

eat three balanced meals

Skipping meals leaves your brain and body tired and underperforming.

eat your five a day

Try and eat at least five portions of fruit and vegetables daily. A portion looks like this:

- a medium-sized piece of fruit, such as an apple or banana
- 2 or more small fruits, such as 2 satsumas or 7 strawberries
- 3 tablespoons of cooked vegetables
- a small salad.

snack sensibly

Aim for healthy snack choices such as:

- an apple
- small handful of mixed nuts and/or seeds
- wholemeal pitta bread with houmous
- carrot sticks
- sugar free jelly
- boiled eggs
- rice cakes.

Make a list of all the healthy snacks you enjoy and keep adding to it. Healthy absolutely does not mean boring!

give it a go

Try making fruit skewers for a fun and healthy snack.

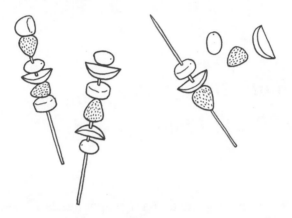

Simply peel (not necessary if using berries and grapes) then slice fruits into similarly sized cubes. Thread on to wooden skewers and that's it!

You can do this with raw or cooked veg too and add some feta cheese.

food worries

If you worry that you have issues with food your school nurse or GP can help – speak up. Your body is precious and what and how you eat matters.

be resilient be you...

...and eat well.

26 sleep well

Without enough sleep, we all become tall two-year-olds.
JoJo Jensen, author

Sleep research suggests that a teenager needs between 8 and 10 hours of sleep every night. But most teenagers only get about 6.5-7.5 hours' sleep per night.

Not enough sleep can cause you to feel less than your best and affect you in lots of negative ways, causing:

- decreased academic performance
- moodiness
- depression
- clumsiness
- struggles with decision making
- low attention span.

Not enough sleep is a problem!

the science bit

There is a clear scientific reason why you might find it harder to get to sleep in your teens.

Teen brains make the sleep hormone melatonin later at night than kids' and adults' brains do. Consequently, teens take longer to fall asleep and therefore need to sleep later in the mornings.

Unfortunately, school/college don't take this into account, and start early, so you have to work at making sleep easier for you or you won't get enough.

For a strong, resilient body and mind that functions at its best, you have to do all you can to get your sleep sorted.

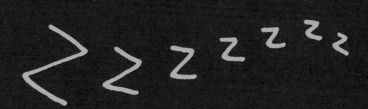

what will help

- Get active and get outside during the daytime so you are physically tired when it comes to bedtime.

- Smart phones and other devices used around bedtime get your mind racing and the light from them keeps you awake. Try to stay off screens for at least an hour before bed.

- Darkness tells your brain to release melatonin, while light from any source stops its production. Keeping your room dark helps hugely.

- Avoid stimulants such as coffee, tea, sugary, caffeinated and energy drinks in the evening.

- Create a relaxing bedtime routine, for example a warm bath and a hot milky drink, journaling or reading. Do this regularly so your body links your routine to sleep.

- Try to have as regular a sleep schedule as possible, and you'll generally find that your 'biological clock' will relearn when to fall asleep and wake up (do this at the weekend too, so Monday mornings are not a massive struggle).

give it a go

Try this guided visualisation when you are awake as a way to calm down, and then use it if you are struggling to get to sleep.

guided visualisation

● Close your eyes and recall or imagine an event or time that makes you feel deeply relaxed.

● Look all around you – what can you see?

● Who is with you?

● What does it sound and smell like?

● How do you feel?

● What are you doing in this place?

Leave all your cares behind and really immerse yourself in this place.

You can go to this place in your mind whenever you need to feel peaceful and content. Your imagination is powerful.

be resilient be you...

...and sleep well.

27 hydration

> When the well is dry, we know the worth of water.
>
> Benjamin Franklin, polymath and diplomat

You may take water for granted but actually it is something to value. Water is astonishing and SO good for you, and here in the UK, it is free and always accessible.

But do you drink enough of it to keep your mind and body in peak condition?

how much should you drink?

Your body is made up of around 60% water and it is important to keep it topped up.

According to the NHS Eatwell Guide people should aim to drink six to eight cups or glasses of fluid a day. Water, lower-fat milk, sugar-free juices and tea, all count towards this.

the science bit

Drinking the right amount of water can hugely benefit you both mentally and physically.

mental impact

Studies show that drinking enough water helps your mood and concentration.

Properly hydrated, your brain produces enough of the amino acid tryptophan which is needed to create serotonin, the 'feel good' chemical in your brain. So it follows that if you drink enough you are likely to feel happier.

Dehydration also causes your body to release more cortisol – the stress hormone. So, drink enough and your anxiety levels decrease too.

Drink up for a healthy mind!

physical impact

Water has also been shown to be fantastic for your physical health:

- it is great for your skin
- gives you more energy
- stops your joints from getting stiff
- stops you getting constipated
- protects you against illness and disease, even helping you live longer
- helps prevent bad breath
- helps you control your body temperature and stops you from overheating.

how to drink more water

- Get a water bottle you love and keep it filled with fresh, cold water. Keep it by your bed and with you throughout the day.

- Have a glass with each meal. Do this for 21 days and it becomes a habit.

- Swap sugary drinks for sugar-free drinks.

- Limit fruit juice and smoothies to one small glass a day, as they're high in sugar.

- Check nutrition labels on drinks – look for drinks with green or amber colour-coded labels.

- Drink extra fluids if you've have worked up a sweat whilst exercising or if you feel unwell.

- Dilute squash drinks well to reduce the sugar content.

- If you don't like the taste of water, try sparkling water, sugar-free squash, or add a slice of lemon, lime, or even cucumber!

- Consider using a water tracking app.

- Don't forget that food – especially fresh fruit and vegetables – contains a lot of water. Eating your five a day will also help.

- Freeze ice cube trays with berries and add this to your water to keep it cold and give it some taste.

There are so many ways to drink more water, and your mind and body will thank you.

be resilient be you...

...and drink more water!

28 move your body!

Movement is a medicine for creating change in a person's physical, emotional, and mental states.

Carol Welch-Baril, neuromuscular therapist

Taking care of your body is one of the best investments you can make in yourself. And one sure way to have a fit and healthy body is to move it.

As we explored earlier, focusing on what you CAN control is what will help you feel stronger, and you can definitely control moving more to build a stronger body and stronger mind.

exercise

When life is tough sitting in your pyjamas eating junk and watching TV can be appealing, but getting moving is a more effective COPING strategy and one that will quickly boost your mood.

Experts recommend that teens get 60 minutes or more of moderate to vigorous physical activity each day.

the science bit

stronger body

According to the NHS, regular exercise has lots of health benefits such as:

- improving fitness and strengthening your whole body
- helping you maintain a healthy weight
- encouraging healthy growth and development
- improving posture and balance
- helping you recover faster from illness and accidents.

stronger mind

Exercise has also been found to produce chemicals in your body that boost your mood, sleep quality and energy, as well as decrease stress and anxiety. It also aids concentration and improves memory.

Exercise is therefore a great way to help both your body and mind!

skill building

Perhaps you scored four baskets in a row, or beat your personal best at swimming. Completing physical challenges and developing new skills make you feel proud and accomplished.

You get SO many benefits for moving your body for just 60 mins a day!

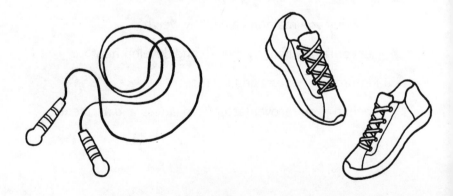

give it a go

The biggest reason people drop exercise is they get bored, so try mixing it up. Can you make a list of ten sports you'd like to try? Here are some ideas...

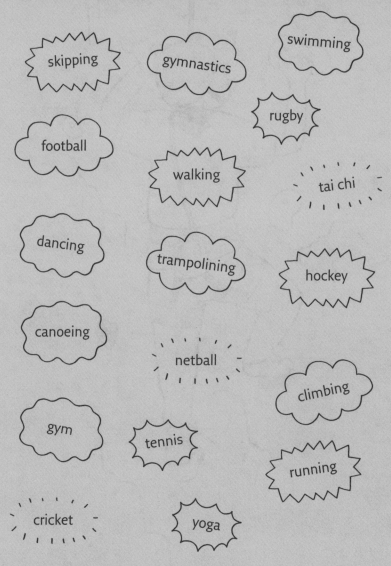

swimming

skipping

gymnastics

rugby

football

walking

tai chi

dancing

trampolining

hockey

canoeing

netball

climbing

gym

tennis

running

cricket

yoga

And don't forget...

- YouTube is packed with dance tutorials, yoga lessons and running tips

- many sports, such as walking, are totally free

- exercising with a friend can be twice as fun.

make time to move

If you struggle to exercise, simply put it in your diary as something you are going to do each day, stating what, where and when. Do it daily for a few weeks until it becomes as much a part of your routine as brushing your teeth.

Taking care of yourself matters.

be resilient be you...

...and move your brilliant body!

29 rest and relax

> Your mind is like water. When it is agitated it becomes difficult to see. But if you allow it to settle, the answer becomes clear.
>
> **Bill Keane, cartoonist**

Get fit, study hard, socialise, stay connected, develop hobbies, plan your future, grow your mind and body, begin relationships, look good – the pressures of a teenage life are immense and exhausting!

It is important to factor in time to **R**est and **R**elax every single day. A relaxed mind thinks more clearly, a rested body has more energy, and both help you cope better with life.

the science bit

When you feel anxious or stressed, you will often take shallower and faster breaths, which will increase your heart rate and blood flow. This causes your mind and body to tense and be on high alert, which only increases your feelings of stress.

Scientists have discovered you can reverse this process by taking steps to put your body into a relaxed state, which in turn calms your mind. This is called 'activating your relaxation response'. It is in your power to intentionally activate your relaxation response yourself whenever you need to. All you need to do is relax!

r&r that really isn't

Junk food, hours of gaming or scrolling, avoiding homework, or abusing substances (such as alcohol or drugs) may appeal as ways to quickly relax, but they don't work and will only cause your body and mind to feel stressed in the long-term.

Always ask yourself 'Is this helping or hindering me?' and be honest. You know the answer.

give it a go

diary in your down time

Try putting downtime on your 'to do' list daily. You might include:

- a walk
- a long bath
- watching a movie
- baking
- playing a board game
- reading.

Your body and mind work better (and faster) when you regularly relax.

take 5

One of the simplest and speediest ways to rest and relax is to breathe deeply. It brings your blood flow and oxygen back down into normal ranges and relaxes your body. You can do this anytime and anywhere.

● Breathe in through your nose and out through your mouth. Lie down or sit with your feet firmly on the floor. Keep your shoulders down and place your hand on your stomach – it should rise as you breathe in and fall as you breathe out.

● Start by counting 1 to 5 as you breathe in and 1 to 5 as you slowly breathe out. Do this for 5 minutes (or through 2 songs).

Deep breaths provide instant calm.

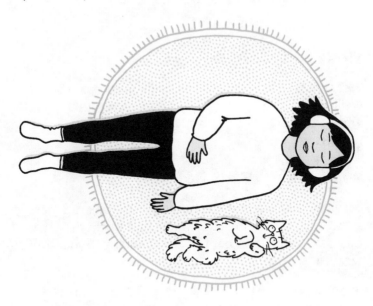

be resilient be you...

...and rest and relax regularly.

30 self care

Self-care is how you take your power back.
Lalah Delia, wellness educator

what self-care is

Self-care is what you do to maintain or improve your wellbeing. Having a healthy mind and body supports you when times are tough, and so looking after your wellbeing matters.

what self-care is not

Self-care isn't hours spent gaming or chomping a massive pizza. These are 'unhealthy treats' that might make you feel good in the moment but aren't adding to your overall wellbeing.

Instead, self-care is a decision to look after yourself, so a fruit smoothie and a game of footie would be better examples of self-care in action.

five more powerful acts of physical self-care

As well as the areas we have already discussed – eating well, hydrating, sleeping well, resting, and exercising – there are many more things you can do to take care of your body and build your strength.

Here are some ideas:

stretch

Stretching is a fantastic way to get tension out of your body and help it relax. Yoga is brilliant for stretching and has been practised for thousands of years.

Watch a YouTube yoga video for beginners and give it a try. The poses help improve your coordination, balance, strength, and flexibility. It has been proven to reduce stress, increase optimism and it's also deeply relaxing!

hug

A good hug is the fastest way for you to get oxytocin flowing in your body! Oxytocin is often known as the 'love drug', as it calms your nervous system down and helps you feel more positive.

Your brain can't tell the difference between a hug someone gives you and one you give yourself. So, if you have no-one to hug why not hug yourself? Wrapping your arms around your chest instantly soothes your body.

bathe

When your body relaxes in warm water, your cells produce Heat Stress Proteins which protect you from stress. Regular bathing/showering means they're constantly in production and this is a super easy way to chill out.

pamper

Pampering your body makes you look better (which raises your self-esteem) and it helps you feel better too. It's been shown to:

- reduce stress and anxiety
- improve physical health
- boost mood.

So, brush your hair, clip your nails, moisturise, get regular haircuts, and put on your best clothes. Use lip balm if it's cold, keep your body clean and deodorise well. Take good care of your body and your mind will thank you too.

repeat

Any physical act you do repeatedly creates a rhythm, which can ease tension in your mind and body. Examples of repetitive tasks that may help soothe you include:

- practising a musical instrument
- crocheting
- walking
- using a fidget cube
- squeezing a stress ball
- colouring a mandala.

What could yours be?

be resilient be you...

...and practise self-care for your mind and body every single day.

resilient
relationships

:)

RESILIENT Relationships

relationships can be complicated!

They can be frustrating and upsetting and difficult to start or end! But they can be brilliant too, and a huge source of fun and support.

As you change through your teen years, many of your relationships will also change and this may feel tricky at times.

The aim of this section of the book is to help you find ways to have more positive relationships in all areas of your life.

Good relationships with supportive people are one of the most important and powerful ways to help you cope in hard times and are well worth working on.

How well you get on with other people is not just a matter of luck, or how they behave. There is a lot you can do towards having great relationships with the people in your world.

Let's take a look.

31 Be inspired (by resilient people

> ## We tend to become like those we admire.
> Thomas Monson, religious leader and teacher

One of the best ways to learn anything is to find a great teacher. Lessons can be learnt from anyone who inspires you and role models show up in all areas of life.

Let's take a look at where you can find them.

fiction

From *The Hunger Games* to *Winnie the Pooh*, strong characters who are brave and reach out for the support they need are everywhere in fiction. You can learn so much from how they overcome their struggles.

Can you think of a fictional hero or heroine that has undergone huge challenges and made it through the other side due to their strength and positivity? How did they do this? What is it about them you admire?

real life – past and present

Real life also abounds with strong characters who have survived against the odds or channel a can-do attitude.

From Katie Piper to Victor Frankl, Bear Grylls to Anne Frank, Malala Yousafzai to Ellie Simmonds – real life role models are plentiful. Giving them your attention and learning lessons from their lives is time well spent. (If you have never heard of these people do look them up, they are truly amazing!)

movies

Do you love to watch movies where the main character wins the day, overcomes bullying, copes with loss, defeats a baddie or just generally turns their life around? *Wonder* is a great example of this and even *Ant Man*! What movie inspires you?

family & friends

Was your great grandpa a prisoner of war survivor? Has your cousin battled health problems but still has a zest for life? Who do you know in your family who has triumphed against all odds? If they are comfortable, you could ask them about their story and what helped them cope. And remember you share their DNA, it's in you to overcome life's hard times too.

Then take a look at your friends, observe those friends who are confident and resourceful, robust and resilient – what do they do differently to you? What can you learn from them?

65% of teens say their main role model is someone they know personally so take a good look close to home.

focus your attention

Your observational skills are key to finding good role models and once you have found them, dig deep to find out what makes them so strong.

Who you follow on social media, who you read about, who you spend your time with all matter. Make sure these include people you admire for their strength, and you will soon find yourself inspired.

Everyone faces challenges, and seeing your role model face their own challenges and bounce back can be a source of inspiration and motivation.

be resilient be you...

...and find your inspiration.

32 hugged, heard or helped

A hug is like a boomerang –
you get it back right away.
Bill Keane, cartoonist

When you have a problem and are seeking support, you
might sometimes end up feeling really frustrated.

Perhaps you want to solve your problem yourself and the
person you turn to thinks you want advice. It can be really
annoying, and unhelpful to be advised on something when
you just want someone to hear you.

Sometimes you might just want to vent your emotions, maybe have a cry and a quick hug, or a comforting arm around your shoulder, but the person is asking you questions and making you talk it all through and you are not in the mood. How annoying that can be!

Other times you might want some advice, guidance or practical help and the person you are seeking it from simply listens and nods understandingly. Useless – and not what you were after at all.

Other people are not mind readers and unless you tell them what kind of support you want, they may unintentionally get it wrong!

hugged, heard or helped?

Jancee Dunn (a wellbeing columnist for the New York Times) wrote an article about offering support called *When Someone You Love is Upset, Ask This One Question.* In it, she talked about her sister (a special education teacher in elementary school) who regularly asked the question 'Do you want to be hugged, heard or helped?' when a student in her class became agitated or overwhelmed.

Dunn realised that this question was useful to ask anyone who was upset, as it gave them back a sense of control and got them the support they most wanted.

speak up!

The person you turn to for support will most probably have never read Jancee Dunn's article, so it is up to you to tell that person whether you want to hugged, heard or helped. Perhaps you want a hug first, then to be heard, or perhaps you just simply want advice?

However, you want to be supported, say it loud and clear to avoid frustration and to get what you need.

give it a go

Next time a friend comes to you for support, ask them if they want to be hugged, heard or helped, and offer the kind of support they want rather than the sort you think they need. They will appreciate you far more.

be resilient be you...

...and ask for the kind of support you need.

33 expectations in relationships

When you stop expecting people to be perfect. you can like them for who they are.
Donald Miller, author

Expectations are what we think will happen, while reality is what actually happens. The two OFTEN don't match up, especially in relationships.

If you expect everyone in your life to be perfect, you are going to be constantly disappointed. Like you, other people aren't perfect and will sometimes get things wrong. They are just human too.

some expectations are essential

You need to be able to trust your friends and family and at all times feel safe and respected. These are essentials and if anyone treats you badly, you need to take it very seriously, step away if you can, and access help and support if you can't.

when your expectations aren't met

It's tough but true – occasionally people you care about are going to disappoint you. For example, they may not realise you are upset or they might forget to ask you how your exam went.

Before you believe their behaviour is a sign they don't care about you, it is worth considering:

1 Could something else be going on for them?

2 Do they know how their behaviour affects you?

3 Were you expecting them to read your mind?

Try asking, 'Is everything okay?' before diving in with criticism or resentment. Accept that not everyone is like you – you might be a whizz at remembering special occasions, but your friend may have a rubbish memory (yet be the kindest person you know).

If something is a BIG issue, explain how it makes you feel and what you would like to happen going forward. Many people are unaware of how they impact others and are happy to make changes.

appreciation

Life coach Tony Robbins advises that you learn to trade expectations for appreciation, in order to have happier, stronger, less frustrating relationships.

Instead of focusing on the negative, make a point to value another's positive strengths and enjoy what they do offer, rather than overfocusing on what they don't.

try this...

Write down something that annoys you about a family member, and then write down three things you love about them.

Annoyance shrinks when you see their worth.

be resilient be you...

...and have more realistic expectations of other people.

34 strong friendships

Friendship improves happiness, and abates misery, by doubling our joys, and dividing our grief.
Marcus Tullius Cicero, Roman statesman scholar and writer

In your teenage years, your friends (or lack of them) may feel more important than anything. Teen friendships help you form a sense of identity outside of your family and are practice for your adult relationships.

But most importantly friendships can be a huge source of strength when you don't feel strong.

friendships change

As you grow, some friendships will fall by the wayside. Your interests and your values change and perhaps you no longer 'fit'.

Don't chase people who don't want you or hang on for old-time's sake. It's okay, in all relationships, to accept something was great once but now it's time to make way for something new.

head for the warm people

When it comes to friendships, it's smart to head for the warm people, and don't worry about being cool.

the science bit

An Australian study found that strong friendships were particularly helpful for teens immediately after a stressful event, such as failing a test.

It's a fact, good friends help you cope better when life is tough and are to be treasured.

conflict

An argument within a friendship doesn't mean it's over.

Strong friendships survive challenges with apologies and changed behaviour where required. Do your bit to work things out – don't just wait and hope (and remember, even good friends have bad days).

peer pressure

Friends who make bad choices (like taking drugs or stealing) can make you feel pressured to do the same. Hormone changes mean you are more likely to take risks in your teens, so you have to be mindful of the company you keep.

Thankfully peer influences can be positive too. Studious, sporty, kind, empathic and supportive friends will also exert their influence.

Use peer pressure to your advantage and pick your *friends* wisely.

how to recognise bullying

The Anti-Bullying Alliance define bullying as:

The repetitive, intentional hurting of one person or group by another person or group, where the relationship involves an imbalance of power.

It may be:

- physical – pushing, shoving, spitting or hitting
- verbal – name calling, racist comments or threats
- emotional – humiliation, exclusion, and coercion
- sexual – inappropriate touching or homophobic comments
- online – sharing photos without permission or abusive text messages

These are just some examples. Bullying takes many forms and sadly it is problem many teens face.

bullying is a BIG problem

Bullying is common, but that absolutely does not make it okay.

the impact of bullying

Bullying can have a devasting impact on your self-esteem and self-image. You might feel ashamed, scared, isolated, excluded, embarrassed and worthless. It can affect your studies, your physical and mental health and your relationships. No one ever has the right to impact you this way.

Bullying has BIG consequences so don't do it, don't stand by and just watch it happen, and don't just accept it if it is happening to you.

if you aren't sure if it's bullying

Misunderstandings do happen and the teen years are a sensitive time. Check their intent if you aren't sure if you are being bullied by explaining how it has made you feel – you may well get an apology. Alternately talk it over with someone you trust for another perspective.

you have rights

Grown-ups would not tolerate being bullied in the workplace, they would report it immediately. If it happened on the street, they would probably call the police. Bullying is unacceptable, and you too have rights. Schools are required by law to adhere to an anti-bullying policy. They can provide support and help to young people experiencing any form of bullying or discrimination.

how to handle bullying

The strength and resilience you need to have in the face of bullying requires you to refuse to accept it. This may mean standing up for yourself, if safe to do so, or getting help and support from adults you trust and those able to take action to make it stop.

1. Write down what happened, when, where and who was involved. If the bullying is online, keep the evidence – photos, videos, texts, e-mails or posts.

2. Don't take revenge or retaliate – it could get worse or could get you in trouble too.

3. If you can, ask the person bullying you clearly to **STOP**.

4. If the bully is a 'friend' reframe how you see them – they aren't the kind of 'friend' you need! Spend your time instead with people who make you feel good about yourself.

5. Report it: Talk to a teacher or trusted adult. If you don't want to do that you, could you ask a friend to do it on your behalf. If this feels too hard, you can always call Childline on 0800 11 11 or visit www.childline.org.uk. Or look at https://www.youngminds.org.uk/ for further advice.

No matter how scary it is to do, find your courage, reach out for support, and let's make this stop.

social media

Social media can feed social drama and spread gossip, causing huge problems in friendships.

The rule of thumb is always: if you have nothing nice to say, don't say it on social media where it can be shared or misunderstood. Try not to react in the moment, and think before you respond.

Your strength may lie in stepping away and switching off.

If you feel left out by what you see online, get off your phone and find something fun to do instead. Take back control.

appreciating difference

It is also a good idea to value friends for their uniqueness – we are all different but are all of the same worth, and difference is what makes the world tick. Difference can make for interesting friendships that bring something new into your life.

give it a go

Write a list of ten things you want from a friendship.

Now look at your list and ask yourself – do I do this?

Put the items you have listed into practice and work hard on being a better friend.

You usually get what you give, so be a good friend to everyone and notice those who give the same back, these are the friends worth investing in.

be resilient be you...

...and remember, to have a good friend, you have to be one.

35 asking for help

Asking for help isn't a sign of weakness. it's a sign of strength.
Barack Obama. former U.S President

During your teens, you will begin to handle more of your problems by yourself – perhaps because they are personal or private, or perhaps because you feel at your age you should be more independent.

But everyone needs advice or support sometimes, regardless of age. Asking for help shows maturity. It's a sign of strength, not weakness. It indicates that you know what you need and you're not afraid to reach out for it.

why you might NOT ask

Asking for help is an admission that you're ready for action and that might feel scary. You might be embarrassed about your issue or feel shy. Doing nothing usually means nothing changes, so push through your blocks. The sooner you ask for the help you need the sooner you can move forward.

how to ask for help

Writing down the things you want to say, and bringing it with you, can be a great way to help you talk through anything that's on your mind.

Be as clear as you can about what you want or need from your helper.

the science bit

A study by a team of anthropologists found that of 1,057 everyday requests for help – whether for information, services, or support – 90% were immediately fulfilled.

People are FAR more likely to help than you might imagine.

signposts

The first person you ask for help may not be able to help, but may well know someone or somewhere that can. Just ask – 'Can you point me in the right direction, please?'

Don't give up – you might need to ask a few times before you get what you need.

give it a go

Make a one-page list of the people/places in your life you can turn to for help.

List everyone you trust – from your gran to your hockey coach, friends to neighbours. Include people who are experts, your GP or school counsellor perhaps, and list great websites and helplines too.

Do your research until you have a contact under each heading, then store your list on your phone or in your diary.

Use these headings:

- relationships
- friendships
- school/college work
- mental health
- physical health
- emergencies.

When you don't know where to turn just look at your list and make contact.

be resilient be you...

...and reach out.

36 romantic relationships

Never dull your shine for somebody else.
Tyra Banks, model and television personality

It is normal to start thinking about and exploring romantic relationships in your teens. Finding yourself attracted to others is a natural and important part of growing up.

Romantic relationships, whether unrequited, casual, or full on, can make you feel amazing but they can also make you vulnerable.

Let's take a look at ways you can keep strong and keep being you, no matter how your relationship turns out.

pros and cons

Having a romantic partner can boost your confidence, make you feel attractive and appreciated. But if you tie your self-worth to whether or not someone finds you attractive you may doubt your value.

It is important your self-esteem is shiny and strong, so in the face of rejection you don't crumble.

keep being you

When you are dating it's important to keep your own interests and still make time for your friends. This will ensure your worth isn't just tied to one person. And, if the relationship ends, you will still have a full life that you value and people to support you and hang out with.

power

If you are being pushed to agree to things you don't want to do, or you are scared of upsetting your partner if you say no, they have too much power over you. This is not healthy.

This may be in relation to sexual things, but also other things, like how loud you laugh or how you spend your time.

Know what is and isn't acceptable to you and keep your boundaries strong. If you struggle with this, ask for help from someone you trust. Keeping yourself happy (NOT your partner) must be your top priority. Think to yourself 'What would I tell a friend to do?' and then do that.

the science bit

Falling in love releases the hormones oxytocin, dopamine, serotonin, and adrenaline. These neurochemicals surge through your body causing mood swings, closeness, obsessive thinking, joy overwhelm and sometimes feelings of anxiety.

Love can be a rollercoaster of emotions, and it helps to keep steadying influences like family time and hobbies going alongside it.

social media

If you don't want something shared online be strong and don't share it online – no matter how much someone tries to persuade you. This applies to messages/photos you might send a partner. Break-ups or arguments can cause people to do rash things.

Being impulsive when it comes to matters of the heart can lead to regrettable actions. Give yourself time to make the kind of decisions your future self will thank you for.

love yourself first

All relationships have ups and down and are worth working at up to a point. BUT if you are not being treated with kindness and respect, no matter how you feel about someone, move on fast.

Less than 2% of people marry their high school sweetheart, so stay realistic and don't let your romance dominate your life.

Loving yourself enough to avoid being controlled or making poor choices is key to the most important relationship you'll ever have – the one with yourself.

be resilient be you...

...and keep your head in matters of the heart.

37 coping with loss

> To live in hearts, we leave behind is not to die.
> Thomas Campbell, poet

One hardship everyone experiences at some point or an other, but is one of the hardest to deal with, is loss. Losing someone or something you care about can make you feel like the world will never be right again and may take every ounce of strength you possess to cope with.

feel your feelings

No matter what kind of loss, whether it be your grandma dying or your best friend moving away, you might feel your heart is broken forever. 'Loss is the price we pay for love.' And it hurts!

It's normal to feel sad, scared, angry, confused and overwhelmed by loss.

You need to let yourself grieve and it helps to express that grief, in tears, through talking, art, music or whatever works.

If you don't have a close friend or trusted adult, you can talk to, look for a loss support helpline and make a call. Sometimes it's hard to talk to those close to you if they are grieving too, so do reach out further.

triggers

Reading about loss might bring you emotions back, looking at old photos can do the same, as can special occasions. You will feel your loss many ways, many times. Over time the intensity of feelings that are triggered will lessen, hold on.

how to cope

If you are mourning your grandma's death, try focusing on why you loved her so much... did she spend hours baking with you? If she did, then bake in her honour, and share your bakes to make others smile and tell them how your grandma taught you.

Keeping the good stuff about the person/pet you have lost alive means they are still with you in part, and this will strengthen you as you experience your new life without them.

the science bit

Feelings around loss have been recognised by scientists to be more intense during teen years when your amygdala, the emotional part of your brain, is super sensitive.

Your first loss can be frightening, you have nothing to look back on and think 'I survived that, so I'll survive this.' Talking to older people about how they have survived losses can help.

other significant losses

Leaving behind a school you loved, or your parents divorcing, may feel as intense as a bereavement. All loss is hard and adjusting to a changed life can be tricky.

Allow yourself to feel your feelings and talk them through. It is important to have space from your grief though, so keep on with your normal routine as far as possible. Eating well, and getting enough sleep and exercising will all help you cope.

give it a go

Make a box filled with things that remind you of the person /pet/school/friend you've lost. Put in things like photos, a dog collar or perhaps a letter they once sent you.

When you feel your memories slipping or you need a good cry, bringing out your memory box can help you feel reconnected.

be resilient be you...

...and accept that loss is hard and takes time, but support is available. You can find support on websites and helplines such as winstonswish.org and cruse.org.uk. You can also talk to a teacher or your GP.

38 giving back

> When you work to improve the lives of others. your life improves automatically.
>
> **Kurek Ashley. motivational speaker**

Contributing to the world you live in is an important part of building resilience. It makes you feel that you matter and are a valuable member of society. This gives your confidence a boost and makes you feel skilful and significant.

When you invest your time and energy into making the world a better place it can make you feel hopeful and optimistic about a better future too, and this also gives you strength. Contribution, giving back, being of service, helping, volunteering – however you phrase it, it helps YOU feel stronger.

helping others helps you

No matter how you contribute, whether collecting for a food bank or walking your elderly neighbour's dog, service to others can help provide you with a sense of direction and motivation during trying times. It's a reason to get up and get going.

It's also true that when you see other people's needs and vulnerabilities, it puts your own into perspective. It is also a great distraction from your worries.

It is powerful to know you are helping improve something and will make you feel part of something bigger than yourself. This not only feels good but will also boost your self-esteem, so it's a great way to help yourself out too.

the science bit

Doing something kind for others has been found to activate the reward system in your brain in exactly the same way as if someone was kind to you. It also lowers levels of stress. By contributing to the world in some way you are boosting your own mental health.

Incredible!

We all rise with kindness.

give it a go

There are so many ways you can contribute inside and outside of your home and school:

- taking on an extra chore at home
- helping your sibling with their homework
- showing new pupils round at school
- being a reading volunteer
- volunteering at a charity shop
- conservation work
- being part of an eco-protest
- assisting with a lower school play
- helping your grandad weed his garden
- going litter picking.

The list could go on and on. What could you choose to do this week to contribute a little more to your community, school and the wider world?

You gain so much from giving that it is a win-win in every scenario.

be resilient be you...

...and find your strength in giving something back to the world you live in.

39 family times

I think togetherness is an important ingredient of family life.
Barbara Bush, former U.S. First Lady

Do you spend hours in your room ignoring your family? Do you feel they don't understand you and make life harder?

Conflict within the family during your teens is almost inevitable – you are pushing for independence and your grown-ups are trying to keep you safe. They think they know what is best for you and you think you know what is best for you. It can cause friction.

press pause

You may feel furious at times that you aren't being given the freedom you want or feel you are not being heard. But, before you lose your cool, it is important to press pause, walk away, calm down and think it through.

Two important things to consider:

- How will you feel about the thing that's upsetting you in a week, a month or a year? Is it worth a big fall out?

- Losing your temper will get you nowhere so how could you state your case differently?

communication matters

Being assertive rather than aggressive gives you more chance of being heard. Try saying how you feel and what you'd like to happen in a calm manner and, where possible, compromise. Avoid being aggressive and aim for being assertive instead.

Grown-up: 'No you can't go the cinema; you went out last night and need to study.'

Your aggressive reaction: 'I hate you. You don't care if I'm happy.'

Your assertive response: 'I would like to go as my friends are going tonight. I can hear you are worried though, so I will spend the next two nights studying.'

Which response do you think has more chance of success?

Listen to your grown-up's concerns, not just their no, and try and reassure them you have heard them.

reconnect

Being on bad terms within your family only adds to anything tough you are going through. Having their backing and encouragement can be a huge support so have a think about ways to reconnect.

When did you last ask your sibling how their day was, or your grown-up, what kind of day they had at work? Showing interest in others takes moments but makes them feel that you care which builds bridges.

the science bit

Researchers at Columbia University found that teens who have emotional difficulties are about half as likely as peers to have regular family meals. It is good for the health of all your family to eat together regularly, communicate and bond.

It's a little thing to do but it has a big payoff.

give it a go

Try reconnecting with your family this week so that you are more of a team. Here are some ideas:

- play a board game
- look at old photo albums
- do a chore together with your grown-up
- bake together
- reminisce about a holiday
- ask them to help you look at college courses.

With small chunks of time and effort your family bonds will be strengthened and when challenges come along, or you need some help, this will make all the difference.

be resilient be you...

...and spend a little more time with your family.

40 your most important relationship

You yourself, as much as anybody in the entire Universe, deserve your love and affection.
Anonymous

The most important and precious relationship you will ever be in is the one with yourself.

Knowing you are valuable, worthy, smart, strong and that you have great coping skills, will help you tremendously in life.

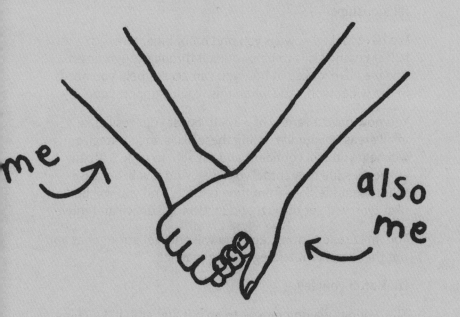

me

also me

Throughout this book we have looked at how you can become more resilient through your thoughts, your actions, through taking care of your body and through your relationships.

We have looked at ways you find more inner strength and better coping skills to help yourself through tough times. And we have looked at how you can access help you need in the wider world and when this would support you.

You now have a variety of ways to boost your resilience in all areas of your life. Using these skills and strategies will help you feel confident and capable to cope with any challenges life may throw your way. And it will, because that's what life does from time to time. And you will be okay, you will get through, bounce back, survive and thrive.

You are already strong, and you will only get stronger as you put these resilient strategies into practice.

Look after yourself.

The world is waiting for you to go out and grab it, enjoying the good times and triumphing over any obstacles that come your way.

You are good enough, you can cope, and you have got this.

... go forth, be resilient, be you!